# AMERICA'S FORGOTTEN CHILDREN, VOL 1

## East Orange, NJ

## MuZ

authorHOUSE®

*AuthorHouse*™
*1663 Liberty Drive, Suite 200*
*Bloomington, IN 47403*
*www.authorhouse.com*
*Phone: 1-800-839-8640*

*© 2007 MuZ. All rights reserved.*

*No part of this book may be reproduced, stored in a retrieval system, or transmitted by any means without the written permission of the author.*

*First published by AuthorHouse   8/27/2007*

*ISBN: 978-1-4343-0775-0 (sc)*

*Library of Congress Control Number: 2007904867*

*Printed in the United States of America*
*Bloomington, Indiana*

*This book is printed on acid-free paper.*

*Cover Artwork by Nate Chadwick of Fat Kat Tattoo*

Dedicated to Mama.

You gave me not only the courage but
the right frame of mind as well.

"If you got something to say, write it down…I can't hear too well."
-Old Man Frank

# Prologue

"Pour another fucking drink, you bastard," I heard someone howl from across the revolting, odorous room. Surrounded by mayhem and cracked walls covered in mysterious substances, I was in South Orange, New Jersey, in the midst of a disgraceful booze orgy. I'd been going to these disorderly parties at least once a week for a few years by then. A friend of mine was a member of a fraternity at Seton Hall University. Everybody knew everybody, and they all treated me as a first-class ally.

I checked the clock on my cell phone; it was approximately 2:40 a.m. I was standing on one side of a beer-pong table with my teammate, Steve. Our adversaries were standing at the other end. One of our rivals was Steve's stepbrother, Justin, who was also a good friend and legal advisor of mine. His partner was…fuck, I really don't remember. We both had one cup left in our vicious gin-pong match. This is a game where you stand on one side of an elongated table and throw a ping-pong ball across the table trying to get it inside one of the many cups containing some sort of intoxicating fluid. If you make it in the cup, your opponent drinks. As they drink, they become sloppy. I highly suggest, if you have never played gin-pong, that you don't try it. It will have any newcomer praying to the porcelain god about two hours later, when all you really want to do is go to sleep, painfully, and have gin nightmares of you and FBI Agent Jake Malloy bare-knuckle brawling in some piss-coated back alley. Anyway, back to the game. Justin and his partner, whose name, as mentioned before, has slipped my mind, had both missed their pong shots. It came to us. Steve missed his, but I made mine. It went back to the other end of the table, and our foes had two shots to try to send it to overtime. They missed both, and Justin jokingly punted over the table of debauchery, which was holding the discarded red solo cups, a pitcher of beer, and an ashtray overflowing with cigarette butts. The table crashed loudly to the floor, drawing the attention of all the drunken cretins that were still standing in that wretched, plague-ridden, bat-sheltering, garbage-filled house we called "Riggs."

The game was over, but in many ways, it had just begun. I took a pull off a blunt that was being passed around the room and then suggested in my slurred speech that we go to the McDonald's in East Orange. It was open twenty-four hours a day, which in my mind, made anything they served a rare delicacy.

"That's a fantastic idea," Steve inarticulately mumbled.

In actuality, we knew how bad of an idea it was, but we were hungry, and at the time, food was essential. There was no force that could stop us from achieving the blissful dream of stuffing our shoddy faces with delectably greasy food…well, no force besides the police. But fuck those cautionary thoughts, we must proceed.

I jumped into the car with Steve and Justin, and we were on our way. We drove down the bleak, poverty-stricken portion of South Orange Avenue.

I had taken this trip many times, but on this night, my inquisitiveness was taking over. When we came upon East Orange, my questioning was becoming overwhelming. I wanted to know the truth about the area. I wanted to know about the mindset of the people. I needed to know about the once-thriving city that turned into a remote ghetto.

It was time to give the voiceless a voice. As much as it should be our responsibility, as people, to give our thoughts and helping hands to those who are in need, it is essential (at least) to present an opportunity to let *everybody* publicly speak. I was thinking about the best way to achieve these ethical ambitions as we continued to drive in environmental seclusion. I stayed silent in the back of the car and just took everything in scenically: the gloomy streets and weakening walls festooned with graffiti tags showing people's names and people's crews, and derogatory statements painted on posters that displayed politicians' names. I observed expressively marooned people roaming the crumbling streets at what was now 3:00 a.m. on a Sunday morning. I was just an observer of these visually poetic images...but not for long.

Before talking with the city folk, it was essential that I research more about East Orange. I utilized the Internet and found out that according to the United States 2000 Census, East Orange has a population of 69,824 people. The racial makeup of the city was 89.46 percent African American, 3.84 percent White, 0.25 percent Native American, 0.43 percent Asian, 0.07 percent Pacific Islander, 2.14 percent from other races, and 3.80 percent from two or more races. People who claimed to be Hispanic or Latino of any race comprised 4.70 percent of the population, which continues to increase as families migrate from New York, Florida, and other regions.

**Other Statistics:**

There were 26,024 households, out of which, 31.9 percent had children under the age of eighteen living with them, 26.0 percent were married couples living together, 28.8 percent had a female householder with no husband present, and 38.2 percent were non-families. In addition, 33.0 percent of all households were made up of individuals, and 11.0 percent had someone living alone who was sixty-five years of age or older. The average household size was 2.63 persons, and the average family size was 3.37. The per capita income for the city was $16,488. About 15.9 percent of families and 19.2 percent of the population were below the poverty line, including 24.7 percent of those under age eighteen and 14.0 percent of those at the age of sixty-five or over.

Now, these are just statistics taken from Internet sites. But my intentions are to go into the heart of the city. I want to speak with the citizens of East Orange; I want to know their views on politics, their views about family, and their thoughts about the future… basically, their expectation of life in general. You can't find the answers to these questions by sitting in front of a computer and jerking around on Websites. Therefore, I had to go into the city. It was time for me to ***be there***. Whoa, that was a scary thought. Being anywhere out of your zone of comfort is chilling, but at this point, it was absolutely vital. It is hard to help any circumstance without visually and passionately understanding that situation. It is not only time for me to learn, but also time for the world to open its eyes.

I made a couple of stops on Main Street in Orange, New Jersey, before going directly into East Orange. I had heard that East Orange citizens occasionally went there to hang out, shop, and eat. So, I would be there as well, speaking with the people of **the world**.

# *Sadistic Sunshine*
# *First Day*
# *A Jehovah's Witness and a Pimp*

THE MORNING DID NOT TURN OUT as gracefully as I had hoped. I fell asleep around 4:30 a.m. and rapidly awoke about four hours later to extremely excited and thunderously loud members of my family. My grandparents were following my aunt and little cousin to their house in Virginia, and the opportune meeting place before starting that voyage was, of course, my humble abode.

I am fond of the night, a vampire child of sorts. Mornings just so happen not to be my thing. I honestly think that I am allergic to the sun. My vocal chords are so rarely in the best of shape anytime before noon, and if I could have screamed like a castrated lunatic when my grandmother booted in my bedroom door to shout her greetings and tell me, "Aunt Dar brought bagels!" believe me, I would have. I opened my mouth, but nothing came out. After some more tossing and turning in my bed, I threw on some clothes and walked red-eyed and grouchy past staring family members and directly to the refrigerator to get some satisfying orange juice. Someone had said something about not being a morning person, but I was too preoccupied with looking out the window for the morning paper. I couldn't see it in our driveway, so I asked my mother if it had come yet.

"Jeff, we haven't gotten the paper for five years." She cackled.

"Good…it's full of wicked lies," I tetchily told her, then chaotically buttered myself a bagel. It was the first time in a long time that I actually had breakfast. People say it's a jump start to a good day, and normally, I could give two shits, but today, being my first day working on the story, I needed just that.

After a car ride full of blasting Tom Petty and chain-smoking cigarettes, I finally arrived around one o'clock in the afternoon in Orange, New Jersey. I was driving on Main Street, trying to avoid a siren-blaring speeding cop car with an ambulance assertively tailing and dodging civilians who were incautiously running across the street, all while trying to find the right place to park. Finally, I pulled into a spot, lit up another smoke, sat back for a few minutes, and just observed. Parked next to me was a still-running Honda Civic, exhaling murky smoke from its corroded tailpipe, with a man sitting in the driver's seat. The man was on the phone and had a look on his face that seemed to be one of dreadful rage. As I was getting my notebook, camera, and my wits together, I looked up to see a man walking on the dilapidated sidewalk, approaching a Hispanic mother pushing her baby carriage. The man was an African-American who looked to be in his late twenties. He was a bit on the heavy side, unshaven, and wearing an oversized black North Face jacket.

Approaching the woman, he pulled his hand out from his jacket pocket and swiftly flashed a gold chain he was clearly trying to sell. She shook her head from side to side signifying that she wasn't interested and continued on her way. The man did the same, while hurriedly putting the chain back into his pocket. This wasn't a suit-and-tie business meeting or a conversation about the stocks…In fact, there was no verbal interaction at all. There was a mutual understanding that if she sought the chain, it could be hers for almost certainly a low price, but since she did not want it, the man was not going to hassle her about it. There is something honorable and influential about interacting in such a subtle way. I feel this notion is superseded nowadays due to the need to fill gaps, even though in reality, they need no filling, just gratification.

All of a sudden, the startling man who was sitting in the shuddering Honda Civic next to me began to scream into his phone like a maniac. I could hear his muffled voice through both of our closed car windows. The dispute had something to do with money. He glanced over to me, and I just nodded. I got out of my car with my notebook and camera and put a few hours' worth of change in the parking meter. There was no need to become part of that flammable situation just for curiosity's sake, even though part of the reason I came to the decision to write this story was curiosity along with the aspiration to somehow bring more of an amalgamated feeling amongst humanity. However, I know better than to somehow provoke a screaming, possibly ferocious and bloodthirsty stranger with money problems.

Now, with no real place to start, I began to walk Main Street and peruse the stores. I stopped for a while when I came upon a striking stone testimonial with integrated children, a pleased-looking family, and a man playing saxophone painted on it. It was a stunning sight.

I anticipated there would be East Orange citizens shopping on Main Street today, so I started walking and gazing at what Orange had to offer. In addition, I was looking for the right time and the right person for my first conversation. One thing I learned working in New York City is that some people don't mind a little chitchat, but some would rather bite the nose clean off your face (which, by the way, if you have the determination is not that hard of a thing to do) rather than talk. I figured having a brawl on my first day of research was an unappealing idea…so I walked for a while.

After about twenty minutes of strolling, I leaned up against a brick wall coated in graffiti that was dividing a women's dress shop and a sinister, unreceptive-looking pub that had steel bars shielding the windows. I was watching the people that walked past me, and the greater part of them did not give the most receptive glances towards me. In a city where the vast majority is African-American, I stick out worse than Bill O'Reilly at a Unite the People rally. I stood at my tattered brick wall spot for eight minutes (and smoked two cigarettes). Fortunately, an elderly and extremely petite African-American woman came up to me. Decked out in a long brown coat with glasses that were covering her entire face and a brown hat with a flower on the front of it, she was geared up for her day on the town. With an agreeable smile on her face and holding a stack of pamphlets, she came over to me to see if I wanted one. *Wonderful, here's my first opening,* I thought to myself as she handed me two different pamphlets. I advanced by telling her why I was on Main Street and how I was trying to get a unique look into East Orange. I asked her if she was a resident of the city, which she was. She went on to cheerfully tell me that she was in her eighties, and she'd been living in East Orange since she moved from Virginia in 1952. The small woman spoke in a particularly soft manner, so I had to bend down to hear her better. She proceeded by telling me that she loved living in East Orange and that she had a couple of sons who lived in the city as well. I didn't get to find out more about her past because I mentioned something about her political beliefs. After that statement, her face altered and her attitude became detached. I rapidly changed the subject and asked what she was doing on Main Street today. She pointed down to the pamphlets in my hand. At that point, I hadn't yet checked out what they were about. One was titled *The Watchtower: Announcing Jehovah's Kingdom*, and the other was called *Awake*. It was about how the end of false religion was near. She cleared her throat and told me, "I'm out here today passing these out because Jesus is the only way, and Jesus cared more about humanity than politics, so the people of Jesus should be that way as well."

I myself have certain beliefs, but at that part in our chat, I felt as if I had walked into a church sermon.

Luckily, she didn't lecture me too extensively, but she did say she didn't feel comfortable with giving me her name if I was writing a "political book." She said, "I don't trust politicians; they're all liars in my eyes. And I'm too old to be concerning myself with all that." Then she opened up. "There's been a lot of tough times that folks had to endure around here," she said with teary eyes. "I'm not sure if politicians…if *anybody* cares too much about the people around here anymore. Like I said, I've been here for years now, and I can't go anywhere. I don't want to go anywhere, really. But these tough times are forming a whole new type of rough people. That's why I just follow the word of God instead of politics." She unhappily exhaled while I tried to convince her it wasn't a political book.

I told her I'd like to get people's political views, but this book, in actuality, was just an outlet for the people of East Orange to speak their mind on anything, but she wasn't persuaded. The rendezvous was over. She pleasantly said goodbye while shaking my hand and continued walking down the street trying to pass out pamphlets "showing the way of God."

The Jehovah's Witness was very nice and showed there were still people in the world getting their word out, whatever that word may be. Her passion was religion, which I think, no matter what religion, is a beneficial love if used in the right way. However, those beliefs can become complicated if you use words to get them out to some when God is not directly in their sights…but neither are the faces of politicians for that matter. My God, then who do you turn to?

After the dainty Jehovah's Witness walked off, I went over to a grimy trashcan on the sidewalk and used the rim as a writing table. I jotted down some notes. In the middle of writing some thoughts down, I looked up to see a guy staring at me, and he quickly turned away. His age ranged from eighteen to twenty-four. He was African-American, and he was leaning his weight onto a cane he was holding. I felt more confident after having the conversation with the Jehovah's Witness, so I walked right up to him and introduced myself. His name was Antoine, and at first, he seemed a bit diffident. The first few minutes of our discussion, he would only briefly look me at me then abruptly look away. He was painfully standing (due to his bum leg) in front of a store that sold cell phones, and he kept glimpsing inside the store to monitor the customers. He started speaking positively about how he was an aspiring rapper from East Orange, but the city didn't have the recording capabilities that Newark did, so he frequently took trips there to record. He compared East Orange to Newark a lot. His tone was spiteful when he went on to say, "There are just more opportunities in Newark…which means less money in East Orange." He lost a bit of his optimism, and suddenly, our discussion ended when he saw there weren't any more customers in the store. He held up a damaged cell phone in his free hand and told me, "I've gotta go sell this shit. Don't leave. I'll be right back."

Antoine came back out after a minute or so, disappointedly shaking his head, suggesting his trip was a failure. He told me to follow him because he knew a man who would want the phone. We walked up the block, which appeared to be a challenge for him due to his limping. I asked him what happened to his leg, and he gravely said, "I fucked it up jumping out the window, running from the cops." We stopped again about ten feet from where we were originally standing, and he went on talking about the police in East Orange. He told me that there was a lot of hassle from the cops, and sometimes, it just seemed unnecessary. He stated, "I understand that their job is to bust up illegal shit, but they gotta understand that not everybody is a fucking criminal…I don't know, man. There's a lot of people in this city that look alike, so maybe they just get confused." He sounded rather defeated. Then he told me again he'd be right back and hobbled into the other cell phone store that was only three stores down the block from the other one.

This time, with a grin on his face, Antoine emerged from the store. He shuffled over to me and excitedly whispered that he sold the cell phone for five dollars. "I could've sold that shit for twenty-five, but fuck it, five is better than nothing." He snickered, cleaned the dry spit from the corners of his mouth with his thumb and middle finger and blasted into an unsolicited speech about existence in East Orange. "It's just a way of life out here, man, you know? Everybody *has* to make money, and that's a fact. I *gotta* find what people will buy. I just sold that cell phone, boom, that's five bucks! Now, I won't be hungry today. I cut my man's lawn last week, so he owes me twenty." He wavered for a few seconds, shook another man's hand that walked past while carefully staring at me, and continued, "Everybody has to be part of something, right? I mean, look at me." That's when he rolled up the sleeve of his red shirt to show the tattoo on his right forearm affiliating him with the street gang, the Bloods. "You see that? But that don't mean we can't be civil. If we could be civil, then we could stop the fucking violence. I mean, I got this tattoo on my arm, right? But I still go to the park and do my little pushups and shit with Crips, and they ain't said shit. I wear my red beads and workout with them, because I know them, and they know me. East Orange ain't that big of a place, ya dig? A lot of people be bumping into each other, and sometimes, that ain't good. But we understand each other, and we don't *have* to be violent…and that could be a good thing for the city. They know I can be all-good, and we can workout together, or whatever, and there don't have to be a problem. But I'm a pimp, so we don't have to worry about shit anyways." He laughed, and he told me to keep writing. I told him only if he kept recording. He nodded and said, "I'm gonna limp my ass back to the crib, smoke a blunt, and stare at the clouds."

The everyday hustle is a burden; there is no question about that. Currently, there are kids with attention deficit disorder, kids that do nothing but fight with their parents, and parents that do nothing but fight with each other and ultimately divorce. Jealously is a commanding embryonic force in our world today. No one seems to be happy for others who are truly content, unless they partake in that joy…or are stealing it. Rivalries start because of another person's happiness, and "deception" is a more widespread word today than "help." At the end of the day, though, we all have dreams, and you cannot deny that. So maybe someday, even if it is for only one day, we can somehow work equally as hard, understand each other, get together, and smoke a blunt. Let us stare at the clouds…and dream.

## *Suicidal Deer*
## *Business is Business*
## *Disturbing Peace*

THE TIME WAS APPROXIMATELY 1:30 in the morning when I finished a nice lengthy and thorough discussion with a friend of mine. We'd known each other for years and were accustomed to hours-long phone conversations deep into the late night/early morning. This is a particularly bizarre thing for me, because in reality, I despise talking on the phone. When the conversation ended, I closed my cell phone, and the house phone instantly began to ring. "What the fuck," I gruffly mumbled to myself, knowing that line never rings this late. It was my older brother calling to say that one of the tires of his car blew out. He couldn't get the damn flat off the back of his car and neither could AAA. "Bummer," I told him. "Well, Grandpa left his car here, and they're down in Virginia, so you can use theirs tomorrow if you can't get the spare on." I hung up and went to my room to read for about an hour. At around 2:30, before going to sleep, I went outside and smoked a joint. I was planning to get up at nine and head back to Main Street to talk to some of the business folk there. I finished smoking, brushed my teeth (which always seems like a lengthy process when I'm high), and got comfortable in my bed. I fail to remember what I was watching when I started to phase out…stories about Al Capone on the History Channel come to mind. Anyhow, I was starting to get very comfortable. You know that feeling you get when you position your head just right on the pillow, your body is just the right temperature, and you kind of feel like you are mysteriously floating off the bed? If you don't know that feeling, I suggest you take about four big shots of NyQuil, lie down, and wait for the magic to happen. You will then know precisely what I mean.

I was descending into that sensation when I heard my mother downstairs in a frantic conversation. "Oh my god, are you serious?" I heard her say. I jumped out of bed, grabbed my jeans and a shirt off my bedroom floor, half knowing that I'd have someplace to go, and came out of my room. My mother held up a finger indicating that I should hold on a second. "Well, at least you're alright, that's all that matters," she said worriedly into the phone. "Where? Between 120 and 117? Okay, Jeff is coming right now," she said into the phone while motioning her hand for me to come downstairs…*Fuck!*

*What the hell is going on? Why now?* My mother hung up the phone and told me that after my brother finally had the spare tire on his truck, he started on his way and a deer jumped out in front of him on the Garden State Parkway, demolishing his truck. "Go get him," she told me. I left thinking that my poor brother had no luck today.

Consequently, I was now driving towards the parkway, still ripped off that joint. I checked my eyes in my rearview mirror, and they were bloodshot red. Already having a DWI gives me certain trepidation when I am sitting behind the wheel inebriated in someway or another. I was reassuring myself that everything would be fine if I just drove the speed limit, making it so the police couldn't justifiably pull me over…or could they? While all these thoughts were floating around my troubled mind, I also began thinking how in another time, I most likely wouldn't have had to be this anxious about a thing like this. However, this is **now,** people, an era a great deal unlike the past, the times that are preparing us to be a great deal different in the future.

Just as I was getting on the parkway, my cell phone started to vibrate. It was my brother, and he told me, "Go to Exit 120, chill out, and wait for the state trooper in the Go Go Rama (a local strip joint) parking lot."

"Uhhh, I'm not too sure that's uhhh…"

Before I could finish, he cut me off. "Dude, just go there! Whoa, this cop is about to shoot the fuck out of this deer, man! Alright, just go to 120."

He hung up, and I figured what the fuck? I couldn't just leave the poor bastard out in the cold. I got off at the exit and drove onto the highway where the strip club was. It was Highway 35, a road riddled with potholes and surrounded by deserted space, multiple adult clubs, and eateries that would seem closed down if one didn't know better. Now, it was my destination for a possible unwanted quarrel with New Jersey's finest.

I parked across the street from where two policemen were bringing my brother. Sitting in my car for a while, I thought of the comical events that could take place between this state trooper and me, while Wu-Tang played softly from my speakers. *"The law, in order to enter the Wu-Tang, you must bring the Ol'-Dirty-Bastard-type slang."*

There was a tap on the glass, which startled me and brought me out of my deep train of thought. I rolled down the car window and nodded to a red-faced state trooper wearing a uniform that looked as if the air between the clothes and his body had been sucked out by a vacuum. "Hey, son, are you Ryan's brother?"

I tried to say yes, but nothing came out. I felt my eyebrows lower, my face displaying a look of distressed confusion. I attempted to smile, but it didn't work. I could feel my teeth grinding against each other. Suddenly, the cop pulled his flashlight out and shined it directly into my eyes.

"That's fucking bright!" I said in a moment of absolute bewilderment.

"Step out of the car, son," he said to me. "You're not fooling anybody."

All I could think about was how at ease I was in my bed no more than twenty-five minutes ago, and now I was being arrested. As I stepped out of the car, I contemplated the fact that court was always an amusing experience, so at least that would be something precious. I put up a pitiable battle with the officer. He threw me against my car and put me in handcuffs. While he was searching my pockets and practically giving me a hand-job to find other drugs on "*my person*," he told me a horrifying story. "You think this shit is bad, eh, son? Well, we just had to send your brother off to the hospital. The officer that was shooting the deer, in a freak accident, missed and the bullet hit a rock and ricocheted right into your brother's ass." He was laughing manically when I asked him if he was serious. "Damn right I am, boy! Tough night for the Musillo boys," he hooted while shoving me into the back of his cop car.

I snapped out of that terrifying thought when my phone began to vibrate again. It was my brother asking me where I was. I looked up to see the trooper dropping him off in the titty-bar parking lot. "Wait right there," I said and lingered in my car across the street until the officer drove off, then I pulled up to get him. There was no need for any of my cruel imagery to come to life tonight.

"They killed that fucker," my brother excitedly screamed while slowly getting into my car.

"I wish I could've seen it," I told him, and he continued going on about how they shot the "horrible" deer three times with a shotgun.

"Poor bastard," I replied.

"Fuck that, that fucking deer destroyed my car. That bastard came out of nowhere, and I nailed the fucking thing. My hood flew up onto the windshield, and I couldn't see a damn thing…just like *Tommy Boy*. Now my neck is killing me, because the damn airbag never deployed."

He was silent for a few seconds, and then I said, "That sucks, man. Hey, you know what, though? It's about 3:40, and those fools outside of Best Buy are probably sleeping now. (People were camped out in front of the store to buy the new PlayStation 3). I have a fire extinguisher in the truck. We could have some fun and jolt those fucknuts half to death."

We both laughed but agreed it wouldn't be the smartest thing in the world to do. I was unwaveringly driving and thinking about the peace I had left, by then, about an hour ago, and the tranquility I would be rapidly embracing when I got back to bed. This serenity was imperative to me, or so I thought. Does peace always have to coexist with stillness? That is a tricky and daunting contemplation, pal. Moreover, something even scarier than the question is the quest to find the answer.

A few hours later, I was back on Main Street in Orange, New Jersey. The merciless street was filled with self-made, non-corporate businesses covering the sidewalks. One after another, they were all right next to each other. In the span of a five-minute walk, you could shop for tunes at the Orange Music Emporium, get a wig or hair dye at Mimi's Hair and Wigs, stop off for some food at Lisa's Deli, and then get some entertaining knickknacks at 99 Cent Dreams. It is like a less fashionable, less lucrative, and less crowded New

York City. Speaking of New York City, I know people say if you can make it there, you can make it anywhere. I understand and appreciate that notion. But I've gained quite the admiration for those who principally exist on Main Street. While watching Main Street's workforce, I see the tremendous struggle seep out of them. There is an intense do-or-die mentality here... There has to be.

> *"So What? We are all businessmen these days."*
> **-Dr. Hunter S. Thompson**

True indeed, doctor. Everyone is out to get that crisp, well-renowned buck. Businessmen, no matter where they fall on the spectrum of commerce, are full of zeal. Their hearts bleed green, and their blood rushes every time they hear the irksome sound of the *ding-dong* bell or particularly when they attain a new client, and so on and so on. I came face to face with an uneasy squirming employee (sometimes employees are stricken with trembling fear, maybe from an unpleasant and horrifying incident from the past, that regardless of whether other people care or not, happens in every area) when I walked into an very tiny eatery called Trinidad Style Restaurant.

Prior to going into the eatery, I stood outside while a woman dressed in a long, tattered purple coat was scoping the shelves for food. I didn't like to interrupt the flow of business by cutting off the customer and asking irregular questions to the staff. Because of my own civility, I waited outside roughly ten minutes, keeping my back to the store, and nonchalantly glancing in from time to time. Finally, the woman purchased something with a hand full of coins and went to eat in the small sit-down area in the restaurant. I went in for some good ol' "Q&A"…or at least the "Q" part.

When I walked in, an older Korean woman dressed in black with dark hair flowing down to her shoulders covered by a pristine white buttoned-down shirt sharply stood up from a stool behind the counter and asked me if I "needed something."

I extensively explained to her what I was doing and asked if I could bother her for some information on the restaurant. Suddenly, she was flailing her hands and her English became broken as she choked out, "I don't know…no, not me…uhh. Wait, I…uh…get someone."

She swiftly walked to the back of the store and brought out an irate-looking Pakistani man, about six feet tall and sporting a fuzzy five o'clock shadow and a stained apron. He came towards me and asked what the trouble was.

"No trouble at all, my friend. I'm writing a book about East Orange, you see?"

He insistently cut me off. "This is not East Orange. East Orange is down that way," he said sternly as he pointed.

I told him, "I know that, but today I'm writing about the businesses on Main Street that citizens from East Orange might frequently come to. So maybe you could give me some useful information about your fine restaurant here." I said this rather hastily, which seemed to terrify the shit out of him. He threw his hands in the air so quickly you would have thought I had a Russian death-ray gun pointed directly at his heart. He banged his hands on the counter in annoyance and perplexity. The scene was getting tense.

"I don't know, man, the boss ain't here. I'm not the boss. I mean, yeah, of course people from East Orange come here to eat. But why do you want to know anything about this place, anyway?" he asked with his hands decisively planted on his hips and terror in his eyes.

I figured I'd ask the enraged chef an uncomplicated question, so he wouldn't freak and call the cops on me. "No worries, man...Uhhh, how long has this place been open? Do you know that?"

He responded, "Seven years. Go talk to the boss. He works at the other store down the street, the one by Walgreens."

I agreed and said I would talk to him and thanked him for his time. I watched him from the corner of my eye staring at me and nervously looking back to his Korean coworker while I walked out of the store. I lit a cigarette and thought I'd be damned if I went on that fatal mission to the other store. I knew as soon as I walked away from the restaurant that fidgety menace would call his manager. It would go something like, "Hey, boss, yeah, boss, it's me from down the street. Listen, some weird guy covered in tattoos came into the store asking all sorts of questions. He was pretending to be interested in East Orange. Yeah, boss, no, boss, no joke...*be aware*. I told him to come down to you, so be ready with the meat cleaver and cut his lips off, so he won't be able to ask questions about the business ever again."

Fuck that…I walked down the street and situated myself outside of a liquor store called Double Dee. I stood there for a while smoking and watching people run up and down the street. Some were running around seeming to have imperative agendas, and some were obviously drugged up, leisurely and aimlessly on the move for mysterious intentions. On the corner of the street, a few feet from Double Dee, there was construction going on. Big mounds of dirt and a heavy-duty bulldozer were taking up the whole corner. Some of the staff were working, some were joking around. One employee put up a makeshift "Do Not Enter" sign on the corner, which proved to be meaningless because during the time I was standing there I witnessed eight people walk up to the sign, stare uninterestedly, jump over it, and stomp through the disorder. When there are no consequences to breaking the rules (or no chance of being caught), no matter how miniscule those rules are, there is no reason not to break them. Hence, I still wander amongst the public.

It was now 1:30 in the afternoon, Double Dee Liquors was getting a profusion of people coming and going to and from the store, some with cases of beer and others with plastic bags filled with assorted clanking bottles. I was leaning against a glass door, next to the liquor store, just scanning the environment. The electronic store, Globe Electronics, which was give or take five feet away from Double Dee, seemed to be the nicest, most well-lit and modernized store on the block, and definitely the spot with the most costly merchandise. A stereo from inside the store was blasting Junior M.A.F.I.A.'s "Player's Anthem," and I waited for the classic song to finish before I went into the liquor store.

Double Dee was around fifteen feet long with enough width for a person to turn around uncomfortably. The store did not have a lot of merchandise for the customers' convenience. The shelves, which almost completely covered the bland, discouraging walls, were virtually bare, and the store was incredibly small.

On my way in, I bumped into an elderly man sporting a long gray beard. He came rushing out of the store walking hurriedly, entirely focused, with his face glowing with hopeful optimism, probably generated from the scratch-off lottery ticket in his hand. It's the hope that keeps us alive.

There was a Middle Eastern man, wearing a white and gold colored silk buttoned-down shirt with a gold chain around his neck and the pendant buried under his mattress of chest hair working behind the counter. Next to him was a younger Hispanic woman sitting on an aged wooden chair, reading a book, but I couldn't make out the title. During my time there, she only callously looked up towards me once then back to the book and remained in that position for the duration of my time at Double Dee. Additionally, lounging on the counter next to the cash register was a wiry Hispanic male in his teens, dressed in all blue, covered in tattoos, scratching off on a lottery game himself.

At first, the three in the liquor store paid me no attention, probably thinking that I was just looking around for some way to reach intoxication. I waited for the Middle Eastern man, who seemed to be in charge, to look up and then started with the introductions. I told him that I'd like to ask him and the other employees about working here; however, he told me that he was the only member of the staff. "Oh, I'm sorry, you don't work here?" I asked the sinewy Hispanic male. He quickly hopped off the counter, shook his head no, took his scratch off, and walked to the other end of the store looking at me warily. Everyone in the store was just as, if not more, guarded and aloof than the workers at the Trinidad Style Restaurant. There was an overwhelming, discomforting feeling that made the walls of the already narrow space feel as if they were closing in on me. There was also a hostile sentiment that if I wasn't buying anything, I should get the hell out of there.

Before leaving, I did get some information out of the shaggy Double Dee cashier, though. He told me that he enjoyed working there because it wasn't uptight. "That's why I've been here for seven years. There's no real hassles," he informed me while sliding his hand over his slicked-back, gelled hair. When I asked if he lived in East Orange, he sneered and spoke in a palpable tone. "I can't live in no East Orange, man, too dangerous." He also said that he commuted in every day.

"From where?"

Well, he wouldn't tell me that, nor did he tell me his name. I knew that he felt I was someone to be suspicious of. "Prime time is Friday. That's when we make out money-wise. Friday afternoon, we'll get some good action, and sometimes, when the night comes around, we see the same people that were here a few hours before. People like to get liquored; I mean, look at the guy right there." He pointed outside to a man in worn-out clothing sitting on the sidewalk curb holding a brown bag containing a bottle of some sort of liquor behind his back. While I was looking at the man outside, my vision was blocked by two men who came in wearing matching outfits with "Engineer" stitched over the left breast. They pulled out two Budweiser tall boys, walked in front of me as if I was invisible, put them on the counter, and started having a conversation with the disheveled cashier. They seemed to know each other; maybe the engineers were everyday patrons. I figured that was the end of our discussion, and as miniscule as it was, I was still content with the overall feeling…even though it was one of distrust. I stiffly waved goodbye to him, he nodded, and I walked out. Business was more important than any conversation with me; I understood that perfectly. The prevalent consensus here with the businesses on Main Street seemed to be that *time is money and you're wasting my time.* The members of staff didn't give the impression of caring where anyone was from or what their life story was. It was a buy-something-or-be-gone state of mind. They had a job to do, and noticeably, that job had nothing to do with a city that may or may not be "too dangerous" unless those citizens were clientele.

On my way back to the car, I saw the Orange Public Library and stopped in before heading home. The library was, of course, quiet and passive. Nevertheless, it was beyond doubt an astounding place; sometimes, you don't *really* realize these things until you've been in an area that is strictly filled with the *grind* and the *hustle* of everyday people. The noises will always be piercing and more constant in a city that is in an unvarying state of urgency.

Initially, the library seemed small and cozy. About five feet from the front door, I saw a round desk where two older African-American librarians were working. To the left was a room with a handful of desks set up for anyone to read or work on anything they pleased. To the right, I saw another wing with three rows of computers and one more desk, behind which a heavyset, attractive Hispanic librarian with her hair in an untidy bun was sitting giving the impression that she was busy working as well. I continued to walk around the round desk in the middle and came to find out that the library was actually quite large. Looking around, I saw rows upon rows of seasoned shelves that were too small, containing the overflowing books. I walked around the different rooms for a while and then unexpectedly noticed that there was a second floor. The library rapidly became extravagant to me. I went back to the computer room where the Hispanic librarian was still engrossed in activity, and just to start up a conversation, I asked her if she could help me find *The Collective Works of Allen Ginsberg*. I actually had the book in the backseat of my car, which made me think of it. She looked up with her pale eyes and told me pleasingly that she'd help me find it. We walked around and searched for my request. She was an enormously kind and obliging woman who went on to tell me that the library was always full in the morning with senior citizens. "They come on in here and read the paper and socialize. It's really nice." She also informed me that about three o'clock Monday through Friday the library got crowded with youthful study groups from both Orange and East Orange. "This place gives kids something else to look forward to. Many college kids come here to get jobs as well. It's a positive place." She said this as we came up negative on the Ginsberg search. I told her that the library was gorgeous and thanked her for her help.

Prior to leaving, I told her about the story that you happen to be gleefully reading right now, and she truly seemed fascinated. "We need something like that," she replied speaking about East Orange. "We need more people to know about what is going on in these areas. There are still good people here, but a lot of negative things still take place here. And it's those harmful situations that make people afraid to lend a helping hand." With teary, pale eyes, she let out a gloomy sigh as she said, "People can only do so much with so little." I told her she was part of the help and that the library was just as good of an influence as any other encouraging force. She wished me good luck, and we parted ways. As I walked out, I felt tranquil. I got into my car and drove to my friend's house in West Orange.

I headed for the house, which we call "The Rock." It was empty when I arrived at around 5:00 p.m. I had a couple of hours to kill before I was going into New York City. I was going to the city to meet with a group of people to hit a few bars. I was not really close with the group I was going out with, but I was asked to come, and I didn't want to disappoint them. The drinking part of it was no hassle at all, but I really wasn't in the mood for any futile, imaginary intellectual exchange.

Once I got myself settled in the vacant house, I tried to read some of my Ginsburg book, but I couldn't focus, beset as I was with confused contemplations. The whole house was empty, and if there was anytime to unwind, it was then. Instead, I walked around chain-smoking, doing push-ups, drinking beer, and randomly staring out the window. I started thinking about the people I had come across today, and I wondered if they were enjoying a peaceful moment themselves. I persistently pondered the thought. Does peace always have to be linked with silence? Is there some setting we are all supposed to be living in that is in between peace and boredom? Is *life* that somewhere in between peace and boredom? I can tell you one thing I know for sure: There is a massive difference between "need" and survival. And sometimes "peace" does not fit into that equation.

## *Addicted*

*Addiction, confliction, yeah, man, it goes hand in hand.*
*Free admission to my submission, I caved in to heavy demand.*

*I need it; I have to have it,*
*It's running my life.*
*I feed it and I feel completed…*
*Now I'm evidently under the knife.*

*The complexity is crazy.*
*It's funny, this started as curiosity.*
*Please do not consider me a casualty…*
*…a stained surgery of society.*
*I cannot escape this style; they deem me vile.*
*It's driving me insane.*
*The need compiles, so I travel for miles,*
*Just to obtain.*

*I need it; I have to have it,*
*I'm too close to the edge.*
*I feed it, I feel completed…*
*I'm addicted to knowledge.*

*I must know, I must grow*
*Please do not go, you must show.*
*Show me how you conquer the problem,*
*If you teach me, I can teach them.*

## *Urinating Scalawags Santa's Helper*

A MENACE HAS BEEN BORN inside of me. I don't know who planted the seed, but trust me, it is there. For some people, my thirst for awareness has become socially unacceptable, and those certain people turn away at the first sight of me...but fuck 'em. If I listened to the incompetent twits that tried to *lead* me in the "right direction," I would be in the middle of a deserted farm selling tickets for the "sunflower maze" to three children for twelve hours every day for the rest of my miserable life. "No! There must be another answer," I eagerly said to myself one day. I knew there had to be something I could do for the rest of my existence here on this world that would keep me closer to sanity rather than madness. I admit, I have had my unwarranted quantity of insane narrow escapes from time to time, but hell, at least I can say I have had my fair share of pleasurable experiences. Sorry, I digress. I was talking about this villainous beast, which I essentially consider my friend that is living inside of me, who is rapidly increasing. I must know, and it is as straightforward as that. I must have anything my brain can get a hold on. Now, I go into East Orange…

On my way there, I stopped by the South Orange Police Department. I had to pay a parking ticket. I was bothered by apprehensive thoughts because I couldn't remember if it had been a month or more since I had gotten the damn thing. If it were past a month, I would've had a nice little warrant out for my arrest, which I honestly was in no mood to deal with. Apparently, you cannot leave your car parked out on the street (any street) in South Orange after two o'clock in the morning without the town's Gestapo tracking down your vehicle and garnishing the windshield with a piece of paper saying, "You owe the town money. Can you please be more of a courteous civilian in the future?" *This is bullshit, damn it!* I wasn't the source of any destruction to the residents…not any that I knew of. Who made these *rules*? That was what I wanted to know. I felt insulted; they should know, apart from the seatbelt, insurance, registration, speeding, reckless-driving, and driving-while-intoxicated tickets, my record was impeccable. And even though this measly parking ticket was not added on to the cluster-fuck of other recorded tickets, I had a reputation to uphold… and this could only hurt it. HA!

Sorry about that; I went on a little rant. I paid the forty-five-dollar ticket then drove through downtown Newark on my way into East Orange. The city of Newark was really on a lucrative upswing. Businesses in the downtown area were already booming, and new apartment complexes appeared to be constantly being built in some parts of the city. I could only hope that the establishment didn't make living in the new apartments ludicrously complicated and expensive.

After I finished driving through Newark, I got onto 280 East and drove toward East Orange. Feeling the breeze squeeze through the slightly opened window and chill my face, I pulled onto Freeny Drive and stopped at a red light. To the right side of my car was a small concrete median dividing the one-way traffic. On the median were standing two African-American gentlemen. They were older men; one was selling newspapers, and the other one was belting out Christmas tunes on his saxophone and accepting any chivalrous tips. I turned the volume down on Bob Dylan's "Masters of War" which was exploding from my stereo and lowered my car window to hear exactly what the street musician was playing. I heard it was the caroling classic, "We Wish You a Merry Christmas" (a vile, overly pleasant song that could make you smile and vomit simultaneously). Even though I was not too fond of the song, I respected the jazzy spin he put on it. The saxophonist's body moved in a constant, slithery sway. He gave the impression that he was only alert to the music and nothing else was of any significance around him.

The light turned green, and I took a left onto Halsted Street, turned the volume of the Dylan tune back up, and finally parked in an Auto Zone parking lot. Directly across the street was a huge concrete wall, decorated in dazzling art asking the citizens of East

Orange to keep their city clean. It was a stunning sight; therefore, trying not to look so conspicuous, I got out of the car and took a picture. I went on walking the street, breathing, seeing, and ingesting everything. There was more seclusion in East Orange. While looking around, I got the feeling of cheerlessness in the city, even though it was around Christmastime. There were small groups of people gathered around on street corners, some waiting for the bus, some just shooting the shit with each other. I continued to walk around and watch the occasional slap-box match take place between friends. I was drenched in the sights and snapping photos until I realized that I was in dire need of a bathroom. I walked down the block to the Dunkin' Donuts and bee-lined to the bathroom door. The door was locked, and I turned around to see one of the employees staring at me.

"I think somebody is in there, man," I said.

"Nah, man," he replied and reached under the counter and hit a button. "There you go," he said while a loud buzzer went off, the door unlocked, and I walked into a hallway leading me to the bathroom. I walked up to the men's room door and turned the handle, but it wouldn't open. I slammed my shoulder into it, and again, it wouldn't open. I thought maybe I needed to get buzzed in for this door as well, but out of the blue, a voice violently came from the other side of the door, "Occupied, asshole!" I paused for a second then let out a wild howl and kneed the bathroom door, making it shake viciously against the doorframe. *Rude Bastard, I hope you were wiping when I smashed the door, and I terrified some more shit out of you all over your hand.*

I walked out of the bathroom hallway and towards the exit. While walking past the Dunkin' Donuts employee, I whispered, "I think someone's dying in your bathroom."

After that escapade, I still had to relieve my bladder. I dashed across the street, lit up some tar, saw a McDonald's, and walked towards it. Yes! It was the same twenty-four-hour McDonald's you could say started this little journey. I had never gone inside the place before. I only drunkenly used the drive-through. But as I walked in, I came upon the nicest McDonald's I had ever seen. It had a nice marble floor and immaculate stone walls with beautiful gold letters pegged into it indicating which section you were in, e.g. BEVERAGES. There was even a video game system in the corner for any patrons to keep themselves occupied while waiting for their chow. After looking around, I walked to the bathroom and found myself face to face with another locked door and a big sign in my eye line that read, "Due to vandalism, this bathroom is locked. Please go to the employees for use of the bathroom." I figured kids were probably tagging their names or affiliations on the bathroom walls, so now they kept it locked. Many people don't recognize the concept of gangs. Honestly, I can't comprehend how people can't understand the notion when the world is run on gang mentality. Okay, let us abbreviate the example and just focus on America. We have Republicans, Democrats, Socialists, Radicals, a party to legalize marijuana, and even a miniscule group called the American Nazi Party...It's the way of thinking that you ought to join a group, you must be a part of something, or, at the very least, you are an outcast, along with the probable worst, you are a ferocious danger. But even after saying all of that, I think people must understand there are differences between political gangs and street gangs. Essentially, a street gang is nothing more than a group of friends who thoroughly protect each other. The gang members rely on each other, and they actually trust each other. Political gang members don't give a fuck about one another; they are the quickest people in the world to shake your hand and smile in your face, only to have your career and life ruined from behind closed doors. Street gangs have order, rules, and are, for the most part, self-governed. My question on the whole gang situation is how do you think the original street gangs were formed? Who do you think were the models to watch and take a fundamental structure from?

After I finally had gone to the bathroom, I continued to walk around for a while. I wasn't actually trying to talk to anybody that day; I was essentially just hanging around. However, just as I was on course to my car, I bumped into an elderly African-American woman named Roselyn. She was extremely petite, had bleached blonde hair, and was wearing an old, beat-up Santa Claus hat. Roselyn worked for a homeless children's shelter, which was on Walnut Street, just a few blocks away from where we were. She had been walking up and down the streets all day accumulating money for the foundation. I gave her the coins I had in my pocket.

She thanked me and said, "You know, I really like your hair; you guys do it so well." I thanked her and advanced by telling her about my crucial research in East Orange. I asked her if she had any facts she would like to give me. "Oh, this town, I've been here for years, child. I was actually in Linden before moving here."

"Linden?" I asked.

"Yes, Linden. I had to move, though; the oppression was too much there. We weren't treated too kindly. But here, it's nice; it's good here. We don't have much, child, but we're grounded, and we truly understand what is important. We might be poor, but at least we're poor together."

I told her I was sorry to hear about the repressive situation in Linden at that time and then told her about my hopes of getting to talk a little bit with the mayor of East Orange. She told me I would have no problem with him, and he was a "nice fellow." I was about to ask more about her feelings about the mayor and diverse political situations involving the city, but she quickly changed the subject and started talking about when she used to have her own company. "Oh, yes, child. It was a graphic design business right down on South Clinton Street," she said pointing in the direction the business used to be. "Yes, we had the beautiful computer set-up, and the business did pretty well. But that was years ago, we were infested with rats in the backyard. They invaded the building and ate a whole bunch of products. That was one of our problems…among many…" All of a sudden, a bus came by and dropped a large group of people off where we were standing. It suddenly became the busiest section of the whole street. We were in the midst of a cluster of busy people who were hurriedly walking past us, some sporadically bumping into me (not caring), and others just going their own unique ways. Through all of this disarray, I still couldn't look away from Roselyn and the pain exhibited in her eyes as she told me her business was gone and there might never be a chance at something like it again. "Well, it's all part of life, child. I'd love to have the business again. I still have the heart and energy for it. But I lost money when it closed down, and other people lost their jobs. It's an appalling thing." Suddenly, Roselyn changed her tone back to a happy one. "And I've been talking to you for way too long. I got to get back to work, or you're going to get me in trouble." I told her that I hoped to see her again, truthfully meaning it. She concurred and told me she was happy that I was writing a book about East Orange and that she was proud me.

I was thinking about that remark later. Here was this woman I had never met in my life before this exchange, and after a twenty-minute one-to-one, she was proud of me. It was fairly weird to me because previous to starting this book, I was talking to a number of people who thought I'd be foolish to go to the city and just start asking questions and think that I could write a book about it. Others had asked if I really thought this story would be profitable. First, I was truthfully never concerned if this story, or I, for that matter, was cost-effective. Now, as I sit here, I realize that it's really not even about the book anymore, either. I've truly been sanctified by the people and will never forget those I have come into contact with here in East Orange. Nobody here has once told me that they thought my idea of writing this story was idiotic; moreover, I don't think they are all gung-ho just because they are citizens of the city. I believe those with whom I have spoken are generally proud of me, generally proud of me being assertive, proud of me wanting to converse with everybody that I can, proud of my actual goals here, and above all, proud that I am addicted to knowing. Furthermore, I am proud of those who want to make a vital impact, even if it is only an impact on one person who needs it. I'm proud of anybody that wants the power to better **any situation.**

## *Holy Shit, Man… Cops Everywhere!*
## *Wanna Get High?*
## *Overcast of Violence*

As I arrived in East Orange, the first thing I saw was a pleasant-looking young couple walking down the street with their hands intertwined. They were enjoying the brisk and breezy, December morning. Who knows where they were going, but who cares, they seemed to be content. Zoom! I snapped out of my gawking trance when one, two, three cop cars went speeding past me, sirens blaring and echoing in my ears like unnecessary and intensely loud techno music. There was always a serious presence of police in East Orange, but since I started this story, I had never seen this much activity. Wondering what was going on, I began walking down the uncongenial Martin Luther King Boulevard, on the road to the same place the cops were heading. I got about twenty feet down the block before I heard someone scream from across the street, "Yo, man! Hold up!" I looked up to see an African-American man, sporting ragged clothes, unkempt facial hair, and a missing front tooth running towards me with his untied shoelaces flopping on the punctured concrete. "Hey, man, what's up?" he asked me as we shook hands. Before I could answer, his tall lean frame let out a small and peculiar spasm, and his next question came torpedoing out of his mouth in halting sentences. "Hey, man! Wanna get high? You smoke? Wait! You a cop?"

I laughed, thought about what I was wearing, which was filthy blue jeans that were ripped from the typical everyday wear and tear, along with a white T-shirt, my extra-large army fatigue jacket, and a black wool cap to cover my growing hair. "Nah, I'm not a cop," I scoffed.

"Cool, man! Let's get high."

I said I was good at that moment and told him I was writing a story on East Orange.

"Oh, shit!" he animatedly replied. Before he could start telling me things, a man came out from an extremely dreary, unwelcoming building that was more or less ten feet away from us. He came out of the door and started screaming at the man I was talking with. No stores surrounded the construction he surfaced from, which seemed to be an apartment building, but there were no labeling numbers on the door. The seething man that came out of this stranded, demolished building was wearing a bloody chef's apron. He again screamed for the man I was talking with. The Wanna-get-high man jerked quickly and turned around to tell the irate man in the bloody chef's apron to wait for a minute. He then turned back to me and just started rattling off numbers. "7432, 874, 25, 8962..." While he was bellowing out these digits, he got awkwardly close to me and started popping the collar on my army fatigue jacket. My interviewee, whose name I never learned throughout this mayhem, continued to shout numbers. I couldn't make out if they were in some sort of systematic order, or if he was just rambling. While this carried on, I put down my collar to see if he would notice…He did, and he insisted on popping it. He kept on rattling and popping my collar. At last,

I realized that he was just listing off the addresses of all the houses that he had lived in before. I somehow also made out through his vigorous and enthusiastic speech that at this moment, he was living on both North and South Clinton Street. "I gotta stay on the move, man." Then he screamed, "They can't catch *me*, baby!"

"What the fuck!" The man in the bloody apron screamed from down the block. "Oh, shit, alright, man, I gotta get going. Remember that shit, though. I lived in Newark till I was four but came to this motherfucker because it's wild, and I love it!" He was yelling all of this while keeping eye contact with me and walking backwards towards the man and the daunting building. It wasn't really walking, though; it was some sort of pulsating sway/backwards electric slide up the sidewalk.

For some anomalous reason, even though our brief encounter only consisted of getting high and random numbers, I felt more of a connection with him than any other person I had talked to in/from East Orange thus far. This man was just out there having fun, getting some work done, and being with the people, and I really respected that. I walked down the street thinking that I would see him at least one more time down this road we call life. But, I didn't know it would be the same day on the same road.

Walking down Martin Luther King Boulevard, which seemed to have churches on almost every corner, I noticed that besides the heavy presence of police, there wasn't much action going on today. As I considered this, a loud roar of a fire-truck siren went off behind me. I turned around to see two fire trucks whizzing past me. I wondered what the hell was going on; it must have been something pretty intense.

I walked for a while, passing only a couple of people who unambiguously did not look like they were in the mood for any sort of interaction. Plus, I couldn't find where those cop cars had raced off to. I turned back around and started walking. Unexpectedly, I heard, for a second time from across the street, "Yo, man!" I looked up and saw my collar-popping friend running like an excited child towards me. "Come on! Let's get high," he said, and we started walking towards the Brick Church train station. He was merrily rattling off some more numbers, this time with no breath in between. "63297052873915570529…you know what I'm saying?"

I told him, "Not really," and without faltering, he skipped to the next topic that was on his mind.

"I gotta jump these trains, man. I jumped three last week! I didn't have no money to ride, but I gotta get to where I gotta go, you know?" I asked him where he had to go. "Fuck that! It doesn't really matter. I just have people to see, you dig? I'm alright and all that, but not much money in these pockets. You need a bag!?" I shook my head no. "Fuck it, baby! I do what I gotta do to survive, ya dig? It's that life! I didn't create it, but I'm here, ain't I?"

It was a fast walk to the train station, and we stopped in front of the stairs that led up to the tracks. He took one more long pull off his Kool cigarette, stomped it out with his unlaced boot, and asked me for five dollars and a cigarette. I gave him a smoke and buck and told him to make sure he got where he was going. "Oh, I always get where I'm going, baby! I'm going to see my girl. I love the little lady, and she love me! Like I said, no money or not, I'ma gets to where I gotta go! Maybe I'll marry her," he said as if he was asking himself. "Eh, who gives a fuck, right? I don't need no ring. I might be crazy! But we keep each other in control. It's a damn disgrace I gotta jump these trains to see her, but you gotta do what you gotta do!" We slapped hands goodbye, and he hurriedly jumped/levitated up the steps to his train. We never got high together, but you never know what the future holds.

Later on that night, I got into an extreme argument with a friend of mine who had told me to go kill myself. Even though he wasn't being serious, it was his attitude and lack of common decency that threw me over the edge. This story had enabled me to see a lot. I have been lucky enough to see that there are still many of America's children living out there whether the nation has forgotten about them or not. Through the affability and kindness, life sometimes seems cheap because there are still people dying. There are people dying from violence, dying from poverty, dying from being forgotten. And when my friend told me to go kill myself, I thought about the people of East Orange that go out and bust their asses and get nothing more than what they were already left with: shit. Then I thought about the people around the world dealing with equivalent problems. There are many people that work hard only to come up shorter than squat.

Life is a gamble. It always has been, and it always will be. But in life, who will **you** be? There are two choices here: You can be the one that smugly condemns others while keeping yourself ignorant and not bothering to find out about what or whom you are ineptly criticizing. Alternatively, you could be the person, that no matter how low times get for you, you constantly provide a helping hand while keeping the bravery to play your own hand…and deal with what's dealt to you.

## Afterthought:

I found out later there was a shooting in East Orange at the same time I was in the neighborhood, which clarifies the serious police activity. I stopped by my friend Lou's house at around midnight, and he told that it was on the news all day. I wondered why the shooting had occurred. I lit up a smoke and just broadly pondered what was going on with the world. Normally,

I would've wanted to know what happened. Who got shot, and what was it over? But, candidly, I just didn't have the stomach to find out. I was close to the area where the shooting took place, but emotionally, I felt even closer.

## *Last Day*
## *Stroll down Hazy Lane*
## *Recollections that Led to Revelation*

IT WAS A COLD MORNING in January. I awoke, feeling nothing but misery, on the floor of my friend's West Orange house, plagued by obscure memories of last night's excessive and abysmal drinking. I hazily remembered only flashing moments of the night before. I remembered when the first shot of whiskey was taken. I remembered walking crookedly into a South Orange bar, smuggling beers in my oversized army fatigue jacket. And I remembered jumping over a chainlink fence on the way home. Why did we jump over the fence?…I don't remember that. My friend's cell phone alarm was blaring the song "Renegade" by Styx.

*The jig is up, the news is out, they've finally found me*
*The renegade who had it made, retrieved for a bounty.*

"Not me, my friend, but all right, I'm awake." I gracelessly stood up from where I was lying and realized I had a god-awful throbbing hangover. *Fuck it, nothing a soda and some cold air can't cure,* I thought while retrieving my rings, chains, and eyeglasses concealed inside of my filthy Timberland boots. I stretched, cracked my neck, and left for East Orange.

I was fortunate today, because right from the get-go I ran into a man who was standing by himself in front of a store called Hood Clothing. He was a sharp-looking African-American man with partially gray black hair cropped close to his head. He was wearing blue jeans with a black flight jacket covering a black shirt, and I was soon to find out, he was quite the poignant roller coaster of a person. I wasted no time immediately introducing myself to him and learning that his name was Morgan.

Morgan was a hasty yet polite man at the age of thirty-two. "I lived here my whole life," he said in a rapid verbal punch. I could see that he was an intelligent man who did not have the appetite for bullshit.

"What're you doing out here?" he had asked me.

I told him about the story and that I was interested in any sort of information or feelings he could give me. "A book about East Orange! What for? Can't you see everybody forgot about us, man?" He said this while purposefully looking at the surroundings. I found that drab statement uncanny, given the title of the book. He asked me what I was writing about, and I figured fuck it, let me go for the neck. I told him it was a book on politics and the community of East Orange. "Politics!" He laughed. "Get the fuck outta here. What politics? Wait, better question, what *politicians*?" He stared at me intensely, waited for a response, and then continued, "Honestly, you think politicians are dying to give us a helping hand here? I'm not saying I need help... from anyone, but I mean come on, look around! Those fucks ain't worried about the ghetto, at least not this one. I mean, look at that Katrina shit, you see how long it took them to get going on that shit, and that was a public issue! Fuck!" He let out a lengthy scoff and then proceeded by speaking on gentrification. "There's cities being revamped all of this country, but you know, there is money to be made with that shit, but the *people* don't see any of that shit. And when they rebuild the ghetto and make some nice houses, they up the prices, and the people that was there before can't afford to go back…fuck that," he said solemnly. "But I chill here. I love it here. This is my place. I don't wanna be one of those guys that bitches about the ghetto, but…" He paused again and then asked me if I listened to rap. I told him I did, and he said, "Alright, take that for example. I like how there are black people taking negative things, spinning that shit, and making shit more positive, you know, a street poetry type a' deal. But sometimes, that shit can be no good. You know, to be constantly talking about killing and robbing, in the long run, only makes shit worse. I mean don't get me wrong, I think it's necessary for some of these other people to really know what the hell is going on in the ghetto, but I also think it's time to grow."

Another moment of silence and I took that instant to remind him of artists like Common, Mos Def, and Immortal Technique. He nodded and said, "That's true, them dudes really put it down. They really make you listen and think about what the hell is going on, especially Immortal Technique; that man is fire. Come take a walk with me," he said, and I figured what the hell?

We sauntered over to (omitted) Street and walked over to the front steps of a house where a group of four African-American teenagers were standing around bullshitting with each other. The group took a long look at me, glanced over to Morgan, and nodded back towards my direction. "Nah, he's all good," he told the group, and Morgan and I sat down on the front steps of the house. The group coolly moved down the block away from us, and I lit up a stick.

It became a gorgeous afternoon, although still a bit cold from the morning winds. But there was less of a breeze on this block which made it enjoyable to just sit around. Morgan took a blunt out of the pocket of his black flight jacket, paused, looked at me, and spoke like an old, cruel wise man, "Ya know, those kids would've ripped the heart outta ya chest, right?" I looked back at him taking a few seconds to think of the proper way to answer that question. I knew if I denied the fact that if it wasn't for him, it could've been a ghastly situation, that could've come off as me being arrogant which would've been no good. I also knew if I sounded fearful by any means, that could've also just ended up in an ass-whipping. Before I answered, he added, "But you look like a kid that could defend himself." And all I told him was that I would've. He leisurely nodded while looking down at the tarnished black boots, then he spit on the cracked concrete, let out a low sigh, and lit the blunt. He took a couple of pulls, passed it to me, and began to speak his constantly-in-motion mind. "It's not a black and white thing. Not anymore, not with me anyways. I can't really speak on those guys," he said pointing to the group of four that were now all the way at the other corner of the block, still gazing back at Morgan and me. "But it is a territory thing, ya know? People get sketched when they see a new face come around, especially a type of face they not used to seeing." I passed him back the blunt and asked him why he thought people's mentality, in general, was like that. He took a lengthy drag, smoke covered his face, and he went on in a manner a lot calmer than the one from before. "In general? I don't know about general, man. I know about the ghetto. I know bout this shit right here. I know that we don't have much around here, and when we feel like there's somebody trespassing, we gotta protect our shit. It's as simple as that, man. But we gotta lot of heart out here. People…and the news and shit might portray us, and other areas that are like us, in a bad ways or whatever. But we know who we are, we know what we got, and we know what we need, ya dig? But if you want clarity for whatever story you're writing, I'm sorry to tell you, you ain't gonna get it. You can't get clarity from people who have real questions but receive no answers. You know what I'm sayin'? I don't know, man, maybe we be territorial because a lot of us feel as if we were robbed…We still getting robbed. The thing that hurts the ghetto is that we not only getting robbed out of opportunities, but we gettin' robbed emotionally, too. So we do what we gotta do to get ours and survive."

We both stared straight ahead and finished smoking in silence…That's something to think about, eh?

I was driving around before going home, and I, by chance, ended up on Main Street. I parked and went into the Orange Public Library to see if I could find the kind librarian who tried to locate the Ginsberg book. She was there helping somebody out; she glanced up at me and smiled. She led the woman she was assisting in the direction I assumed she needed to go and came up to me asking if I had found "that, uh, *Ginsberg book*?" I was surprised she remembered and told her that I did find it. She asked if she could help me out with anything else. I told her I was fine, and I was just getting out of the cold. She smiled and told me the finest thing I had heard in a while. "Okay then, well good luck on that book you're writing." I was taken back, but I managed to peep out a thank you. It was then I realized that this book has the potential to mean something to somebody other than me.

I remember leaving the library feeling rejuvenated and just wanting to finish this story and get it out to anybody that would read it. Even though I did not get the chance to meet with the mayor, I feel blessed, due to the city of East Orange, with a rather large invigorating and influential shock that brought me back to life. The things I have seen, the people I have met, and the words I have heard I will never forget. I can only hope that you, not only the *reader*, but also the ***person,*** as well, will always remember.

# *CHECKMATE*

*AMERICA'S REBELS HAVE BEEN SNIFFED OUT, discovered, and destroyed, America's kiss-asses pushed aside, lives seized without any real judgment. Ignorance runs continually with constant bigotry. The narrow-mindedness is the open-eyed, all-seeing blindness. Lies and greed will make the blackest heart bleed. I have observed the alleged fight for freedom, prosperity, and equality, but I have yet to witness any one of the major players get their hands "dirty." Tupac Shakur once said something along the lines that the homeless weren't always homeless, they have ideas as well. However, some politicians cannot see that; once again, they are too afraid to get their hands "dirty." They continue to sit in prominent offices, with immaculate surroundings. How can **you** tell **me** what is going on with **my** life? How can* *you fix the problems of the world, if **your** world does not intermingle with **ours**? Instead of gazing out the windows, stare into the eyes of America's children; I dare you to look into our souls. If I go to bed hungry, I will steal food in the morning. If I have bills to pay while I am on minimum wage, I will steal money to make my payments. It seems to be inflexible lunacy; we could never truly understand every political element. The conspiracies alone would blow our mind, but please...let us grasp the facts. How could you ever expect the truth and live in contentment while surrounded regularly by lies?*

*Are we political pawns just waiting to be defeated? Checkmate...how do you think money generates? Where do you think the guns come from? The omnipotent eye in the sky is no longer the lord. Every word I speak and every phrase I write is being broken down and analyzed. Billions of our dollars are spent to make sure that we "live" secure. Those same people that keep us "sheltered" will kill you over the protection of their so-called security. Talk about taking a secret to the grave.*

*So now what do we fight for? Whom do we look up to? Who will be our role models? Do we stand up and preach or sit down in silence? It's hard to cope; will they even take note if we begin to speak? Shit, are there no more world-shattering heroes? The answers are within the truth. It is a shame society will pay the price for a proper life...and ultimate death.*

*So throw your bets down. It is one for all and all for one. We are supposed to be a nation united...correct? What a wonderful notion! The embarrassing actuality is that's where it all ends, just as a concept. In addition, always remember a mind is a horrible thing to waste. Without your own train of thought, you are nothing but another pawn amongst kings.*

*Checkmate!*

VOL. 2 IS BEING BUILT

Printed in the United States
89086LV00001B/49/A